Text copyright © Michael Hardcastle 1999
Illustrations copyright © Chris Leishman 1999

First published in Great Britain in 1999
by Macdonald Young Books
an imprint of Wayland Publishers Ltd
61 Western Road
Hove
East Sussex
BN3 1JD

Find Macdonald Young Books on the internet at
http://www.myb.co.uk

The right of Michael Hardcastle to be identified as the author
and Chris Leishman as the illustrator of this Work has been
asserted by them in accordance with the
Copyright, Designs and Patents Act 1988

Designed by Leishman Design
Printed and bound by Guernsey Press

British Library Cataloguing in Publication Data available

ISBN: 0 7500 2793 2

Striker's Boots

MICHAEL HARDCASTLE

Illustrated by Chris Leishman

MACDONALD YOUNG BOOKS

Chapter One

"Right, Sean, you're definitely playing for the school today. So make sure you have a great game," Mr Halbury announced in front of the entire class.

"But – but – but—" Sean tried to reply.

Mr Halbury was grinning. "Now come on, Sean. No excuses. You've been angling for a place in the team for long enough. Well, now you've got it! Don't tell me you've changed your mind?"

"But I haven't got my boots with me," Sean managed to get out. "I mean, I didn't think you'd be picking me, Mr Halbury. Yesterday you said the team had picked itself and I wasn't in it."

"Ah, well, nothing stays the same for ever, does it, Sean? The point is, Tony forgot to tell me he has a dental appointment straight after school. So he's losing a tooth and I'm losing a striker. But at least you're gaining something – a game you didn't expect…"

"Yes, but—"

"…so I'm looking for a really good game from you, Sean," went on the teacher unstoppably.

"I'll play brilliantly as long as I've got my boots," promised Sean, lifting up his feet. "I can't play in these."

His old black trainers really did look as if they might disintegrate if they ever kicked a ball. Mr Halbury nodded. "In that case, you have my permission to sprint home at dinner-time to collect the real things. Just don't use up all your energy. Scotney will be all over us from the start. They are the fittest team I've seen all season."

"Sean can borrow my boots if he likes," said Simon. He would say and do anything to please Mr Halbury.

"I think he'll play best in his own boots just as long as he can get hold of them quickly," replied the teacher "But thanks for the offer, Simon."

"That's OK, sir" said Simon, smugly. Everyone in the class rolled their eyes up or turned their thumbs down or did both. Simon didn't notice them, just as he never seemed to notice that Mr Halbury hated to be called "sir".

The bell signalled dinner-time and Sean was darting for the door when Simon stopped him. "I meant what I said about my boots, you know. I think I should have been picked in Tony's place. But I support the team, man, so if the boss chooses you, I go along with it."

"Terrific!" replied Sean. He didn't mean it but there wasn't time to waste on Simon. If he could get home and back in record time he might still manage a school dinner. And Bazby school dinners were always in the Premier League.

Chapter Two

Sean lived in Smugglers' Lane which had probably never seen a smuggler in its history. By the time he reached his house he was out of breath because he'd run nearly all the way.

All the houses in the lane were set apart so when Sean found both front and back doors locked, his first idea was to break a window to get in. But then he'd have to admit to the crime, and his mum would stop his pocket money for weeks. He was already in debt to her after smashing a window accidentally with a baseball.

He sat on the garden seat and tried to work out what to do. He was desperate but he knew he mustn't do anything completely stupid.

Getting into the school team was the most important ambition of his life. He'd waited for a long time for his chance because Mr Halbury disliked changing a winning team. And lately, Bazby's record had been perfect.

Sean decided to make another circuit of the house to see whether any windows were open. Suddenly he had an idea. Mrs Kitchen might have a key to the house! When Sean's family were away, their neighbour, Mrs Kitchen came in to water the plants and pick up the post. So…

He darted round to her house and felt like cheering when she answered his furious ringing at the door. "Hello, Sean," she said cheerfully. "Funny time to see you. Something wrong at school?"

"No, nothing like that. I just need to get into the house. Can I borrow your key for a minute?" Then, remembering how she fussed about politeness, he added "Please".

"Ah. That could be a problem. I promised your mum I'd never let that key touch another person's hands. Can't break a solemn promise, can I?"

"But I live there!" Sean pointed out.

"Oh, I know that, Sean. But you see, if your mum had wanted you to have a key she'd have given you one, wouldn't she?' Mrs Kitchen spoke in a triumphant voice.

"But, all I want is my football boots. I need them desperately to play for the school in a really big match. I won't take anything else from the house, I promise, Mrs Kitchen!" Sean thought it was terrible that he had to plead like this to get into his own home. But he knew that Mrs Kitchen had funny ideas about what children should and shouldn't be allowed to do.

"What time is this big match?" she asked unexpectedly.

Thinking that he might get round her after all Sean replied: "Oh, straight after school. It's on our field and—"

"Well, your mum will be home long before that. She can get your boots to you in good time," Mrs Kitchen said, patting her grey hair. "In fact, she should be home in about an hour. She's normally finished her shift at the hospital by two o'clock. That's ample time for her to bring the boots up to school. If that's what you really want out of the house, that is," she added darkly.

Sean was beginning to feel trapped. He could sense his chances of playing for the school slipping away. "But I can't ring Mum or anything, can I?" he said desperately. "She can't take phone calls at work, and I can't phone from school."

"Ah, well, the answer to that little problem is simple," smiled his cunning neighbour. "You can leave her a note. Just push it through the letterbox and she'll find it on her return.

It was a solution, Sean could see that. "But I haven't got a pen or —"

"No problem!" interrupted Mrs Kitchen. "I'll lend you a pencil and notepaper." He would have followed her into the house but she didn't give him the chance. She even half-closed the door on him when she turned away. What was she worried about? Did she

think he'd spy on her or steal something? Sean
sighed. He wasn't the slightest bit interested in
her or her house – he just wanted his football
boots!

"There you are," she said, handing over a
pencil and note pad. "Be very neat now." She
peered over his shoulder as he leaned the pad
against the doorpost.

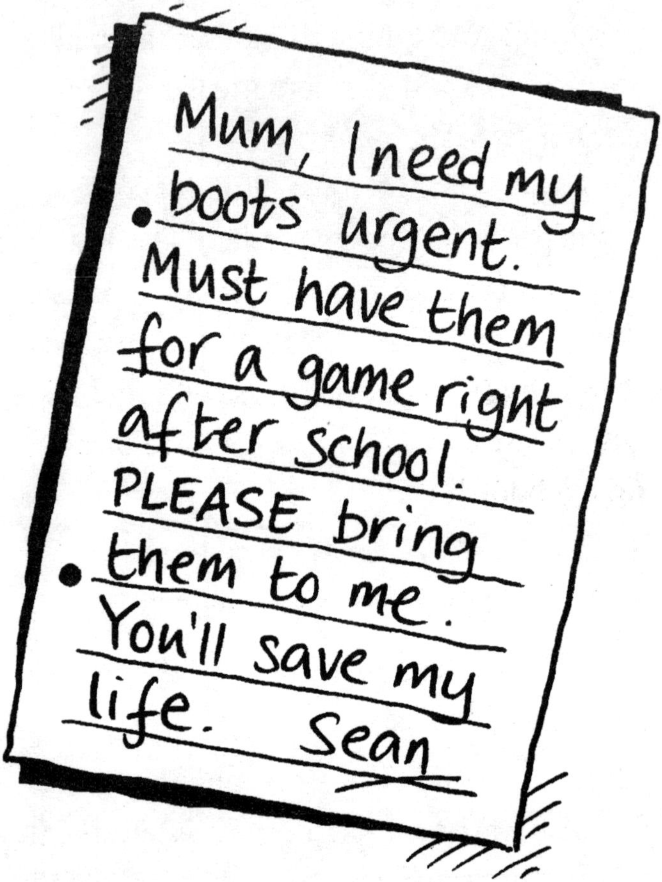
Mum, I need my
boots urgent.
Must have them
for a game right
after school.
PLEASE bring
them to me.
You'll save my
life. Sean

"I think you should have written 'urgently,' not 'urgent'. Don't they teach you grammar at your school? And I don't think that football boots can be regarded as a matter of life and death. Really, Sean!"

He wasn't going to argue. Simply handing back the pencil and pad he called "Thanks!" and raced down the path round to his own house. Pushing the folded note through the letterbox, he stood with his fingers crossed and said aloud: "Mum, please come home quick! And please bring my boots!"

Chapter Three

Although he managed to run most of the way back to school Sean wasn't in time for the best dinners; they'd all gone. He wasn't keen on cheese flan because his mum didn't eat meat and they all ate plenty of vegetarian food at home.

Still, he needed something so he ate it with a portion of chips (his mum wouldn't have approved of chips, either). At least she wouldn't have complained about the banana he took for pudding. Bananas were energy food and he would need all the energy he had when the match started.

Before the bell went for the first lesson of the afternoon he joined in a kickabout on the edge

of the sports field. But even then things just
seemed to go wrong. When he took a mighty
kick at the ball to send it back to the goalkeeper,
his shoe flew off. What was worse, when he
picked it up he found it had split. His fears
about his flimsy footwear had been all too real.

"If your football boots are as bad as those you'll end up scoring own goals in bare feet!" jeered Simon, who had seen everything of course.

Sean ignored him. But as he went back to his classroom he couldn't get rid of the feeling that this was his unlucky day – the day he was picked for the team and yet the day everything else went wrong.

"Got those top striker's boots of yours?"

Mr Halbury asked as soon as he'd marked the register. "Er, no, my mum's bringing them later," Sean replied, fingers crossed.

"I'm ready to play, sir, if you need me," Simon piped up.

To Sean's relief the teacher ignored Simon and got on with the lesson. Sean wasn't particularly interested in minibeasts and plant life but he tried to pay attention.

The nearest window gave Sean a view of the school entrance and he couldn't help keeping a lookout. If only he could catch sight of Mum arriving, he'd know he was certain to play. He couldn't think about anything else.

"If you look out of that window again, Sean, you'll go and stand in the corridor," said Mr Halbury cutting through his dreams. "Then the Head will know you've been up to no good and probably ban you from football for life!"

"Sorry!" gasped Sean. He knew the threat was a bit over the top but there was still a chance the Head would ban him from today's match, however much the school needed a full team.

So he didn't see his mum arrive half-an-hour before school finished. She wasn't in the best of moods and she was in a hurry. She simply dumped a plastic bag in the secretary's office and asked that it be handed over to Sean. Her day had been difficult enough already, and now she had to pick up Sean's step-brother from his school and take him to a trumpet lesson. One day, she told herself as she drove away, her family would run around for her.

"Oh great!" Sean exclaimed when the secretary kindly delivered the boots to him just before the final bell. "Thanks, Mum!" he breathed silently.

But two minutes later he was wailing: "Oh no! Oh, Mum, how could you? How could you do something as terrible as this?"

Chapter Four

The boots were not his; they belonged to his step-brother, Will. Although Will was only a year older, his boots were much, much bigger than Sean's. They were clean and shining and looked as good as any soccer boots Sean had ever seen. But they were too big! He'd never be able to play properly in them.

All the same, he put them on because he had
no choice. Somehow he'd have to find a way of
using them so they didn't fly off his feet when
he kicked the ball.

"OK, Sean? You look a bit worried," said
Mr Halbury as he walked round the changing
room, handing out the school's green-and-
yellow shirts.

"Yeah, I'm fine, Mr Halbury," Sean replied,
not daring to tell the truth. If he missed this
match he might never get another chance of
playing for Bazby again.

Liam, Bazby's captain, was combing his thick, shiny black hair. It didn't seem to matter that it would get messed up as soon as he headed the ball. He wanted to look his best at all times in case, he said, a newspaper photographer was at the match. "The captain of Bazby School Soccer Eleven has to look like a leader," he always said. Mr Halbury said that Liam was a perfectionist. Sean wished that just one thing could be perfect for him – his boots.

"You'll be playing up front with me Sean,"
Stewart pointed out as they left the changing-
room. "Remember I'm the star player, so keep
passing the ball to me."

Sean had never known Stewart boast like this
before. But because all he could think about
were his boots, he wasn't going to say it. Even so,
he'd never heard such rubbish. All players were
equal when a team was on the pitch.

The Scotney players, in red-and-black striped shirts, looked as fit as Mr Halbury had described. Sean wondered how good he'd be at climbing high for any crosses from the wing. Would the big boots hold him down? They felt like flippers. He was sure he was going to trip up after every step he took. Yet somehow he managed to remain upright as Bazby practised shooting and short passing before the kick-off.

"Listen, this lot'll try to overrun us from the start, so it's our job to attack them," Mr Halbury told the team. "Sean, this is your big chance. Take it – and give us some goals to remember!"

Sean wished Mr Halbury hadn't said that. He felt as if he'd have difficulty in running into position let alone hitting goal-bound shots. If he turned out to be a complete flop he'd lose Bazby the match and Mr Halbury would never forgive him. Neither would his team-mates. Just before the kick-off he fastened his laces yet again, tighter than ever. And this time the boots did feel a bit better. Perhaps he'd be able to manage after all.

"Yours, Sean!" Liam was calling within moments of the kick-off. He'd won possession and was sliding the ball cleverly past an opponent and into Sean's path. It was exactly the sort of pass a top striker dreamed about. If he could convert it into a successful strike he'd be on top of the world.

Sean darted forward, eager to make a run. He got to the ball but knew he was moving clumsily. His feet felt as if they were in wellington boots.

So he wasn't surprised when a defender came at him quickly, trying to poke the ball away. Luckily, Sean just managed to push it sideways to Stewart. But Stewart made a mess of trying to turn an opponent and the ball was lost.

"You've got to move a bit faster than that, Sean!" Mr Halbury called from the touchline. Sean pretended that he hadn't heard. He thought it was mean of Mr Halbury to criticize when Stewart hadn't done any better.

But next time he had the ball, Stewart moved like lightning, cutting inside past two defenders and then sending in a stinging shot. However, he had little hope of beating the goalkeeper from that range, especially one as good as Scotney's. Alan was a star in his own right, also playing for top junior side Linkslade Lions. Alan pulled the ball down easily, looked for a team-mate and threw it accurately to set up a Scotney attack.

"You could have passed to me there," Sean told his fellow striker. "I mean, I was in a good position to get close in and really beat the goalie."

"Never saw you," Stewart replied quickly. Sean didn't believe him but he was in no position to argue. After all, he'd been criticized in front of everyone by the team boss.

Within five minutes the opposition had gone ahead. This time it was Liam who made a mistake, miskicking on the edge of the penalty area. Scotney's tall, fair-haired centre-forward pounced on the loose ball, jinked sideways and slid it into the net just inside the far post.

While Liam covered his face with his hands in shame Mr Halbury threw his arms up into the air as if to say, "What sort of idiots have I got playing for me?"

Only six more minutes had passed when Sean was in trouble again. By then Liam had fully recovered and kept urging his team-mates to "Chase, chase, chase! Get the ball for us!"

Sean, eager to get back into the game, did as he was told. He ran as fast as he could to catch up with a Scotney midfielder. Even before he reached his opponent Sean felt his right boot come loose; it started to flap. Then, when he tried to slide in for a tackle, it fell off completely and Sean fell over, practically turning a somersault. Some spectators laughed out loud. Mr Halbury turned pink and then red. "Sean!" he yelled. "What d'you think you're playing at? Tap dancing?"

Chapter Five

Even the ref was smiling as he waved play on. Sean came off the pitch. His face was now as red as the stripes on Scotney's shirts as he struggled to lace up his right boot. He was near enough to the touchline to reply to his teacher's question. "Sorry, Mr Halbury," he said, "but these boots are just too big. They're Will's, my brother's. He's a striker but he's bigger—"

Mr Halbury didn't care whose boots they were if they weren't any good. "Well, you've got to change 'em. You can't kick properly in your socks!"

It was then that the ever-helpful Simon renewed his offer. He was, of course, standing beside his teacher when he said: "Go on, Sean, take my boots. You can't do any worse in them." He was smiling quite innocently as he spoke.

Sean was too desperate to worry about that remark. "Thanks," he mumbled, holding out his hands for the very smart boots.

It was a struggle to get into them and Mr Halbury crossly told Sean to hurry up. "We're down to ten men while you get your boots on," he pointed out.

Then he turned to Simon." That was very sporting of you, Simon," he said. "Very generous."

"Oh, I'd do anything for our team, sir," Simon replied smugly.

As soon as he started running Sean felt the tightness around his toes. Biting his lip to keep the discomfort at bay he went for the ball the moment it came near him.

To his relief he was able to trap it, turn and then fire a good pass to Stewart. And Stewart quickly fed it to Liam, who tried a snap shot which brought the best out of the goalkeeper. Alan had to dive almost full-length to keep the ball out of the net.

"That's better, Sean, much better," the boss applauded. The encouragement cheered him up – and he badly needed it. Ever since putting them on, Simon's boots seemed to have shrunk. Now, they were biting him all round the foot.

The pain was getting worse almost every time he moved. Sean had decided this must be the unluckiest day of his entire life!

Just as Sean was wondering whether it might be an idea to get himself injured in a tackle, Bazby scored. It was Liam who set things in motion, bringing in Paul, a full back who loved to raid down the wing. Paul put over a perfect cross, Sean jumped and got his head to it, knocking the ball down, and even the brilliant Alan couldn't keep out Stewart's fierce drive.

Sean forgot his pain and he and his team-mates hugged in delight. That goal kept him going until half-time.

"Those boots are no good for you, are they?" Mr Halbury asked him as the players drank orange squash. "Much too small."

"How do you know that?" Sean gasped. He hadn't wanted to complain in case Mr Halbury was so fed up he sent a sub on in Sean's place.

"I do watch a lot of football, Sean, so I have some idea what's happening to players," he said with his favourite superior expression. "If you can't run, you can't play. But if we put some stuffing in your brother's boots they might fit you after all. Simon, you've got small feet and you're wearing thin socks. I need 'em – the socks I mean."

"What?" asked Simon, shocked by this unexpected demand.

"Come on. You said you'd do anything for the team. Well, you're getting your boots back and when the game's over you'll get the socks back too."

"Yes, sir," said Simon, faintly, reluctantly taking them off.

"Might smell a bit when they're returned," grinned Mr Halbury, rolling them up and pushing them as tightly as possible into the toes of Will's boots.

"But you won't notice that because you'll be wearing them! There you go, Sean, try these for size."

"Great Mr Halbury, just great!" enthused Sean when he did so. The boots were a perfect fit. He jumped up and down on the spot, and practised a couple of sharp sprints. He beamed at Simon, but got only a frown in return.

By the time he was back on the pitch for the second half, Sean's only thought was to score. He felt he had enough energy for the entire team. And no one ran faster, or worked harder for Bazby. His team-mates quickly got caught up in the excitement when he sparked off and another sword-like thrust from Paul led directly to Bazby's second goal. The full-back was sent sprawling in the box. When the ref signalled a penalty Liam converted the kick with ease.

After going behind, Scotney seemed to wilt. With only five minutes to go before the final whistle, Bazby scored the goal that would put the result beyond doubt. This time it was Sean who started the move – and Sean who finished it off.

After sending a precise pass to Daniel, and calling for the return he raced into the penalty area. But Stewart reached the ball ahead of him and blasted in a fierce shot. For once, Alan couldn't hold it and Sean was there to slip the rebound into the net before the goalie could recover. At the same time, the piercing sound of the final whistle shrilled in his ears.

Even as the players left the field Sean was still glowing with pleasure.

"Good goal, Sean, well played," Mr Halbury said, congratulating him with a hug.

"It was only a tap-in," Sean said with his usual honesty.

"Ah, but it was a real striker's goal. Scored because you were in the right spot at the right time," his teacher declared. Then, with a grin, he added, "After all you were wearing a striker's boots!"

Read more of Michael Hardcastle's soccer stories:

SOCCER SECRET

Tom is a brilliant striker and he likes nothing better than
boasting about all the goals he scores.
What he doesn't know is that his cousin, Alan
is good at football too – as a goalie.
When will Alan get the recognition he deserves,
without upsetting Tom?

INJURY TIME

Joe would be a really good player, if he weren't so
accident-prone. He always seems to be suffering
from aches and pains and rarely gets
through a match without injury.
The coach thinks that he's a fake, but Amy's not sure.
Could there be another reason for Joe's problem?

RIVALS UNITED

When East End's star striker defects
to the West End team, his team-mates can't believe it.
Just what does David think he's playing at?
Then there's a local derby when the two teams meet.
The winning side could be promoted to league status,
but where do David's loyalties lie?

For more information about Mega Stars,
please contact: The Sales Department,
Macdonald Young Books,
61 Western Road, Hove,
East Sussex BN3 1JD